MW01526345

Predators of Shark River

by Dr. Michael R. Heithaus

HOUGHTON MIFFLIN HARCOURT

PHOTOGRAPHY CREDITS: COVER ©Stockbyte/Getty Images; 3 (br) ©Michael Heithaus; 3 (bl) ©Rudy Umans/Shutterstock; 4 (br) ©Michael Heithaus; 4 (tr) ©Michael Heithaus; 7 (b) ©Michael Heithaus; 9 (cr) ©Andrew Fritz; 10 (br) ©Michael Heithaus; 10 (tr) ©Adam Rosenblatt; 11 (tr) ©Jeffery Rauch; 12 (cr) ©Michael Heithaus; 14 (b) ©Michael Heithaus

Printed in Mexico

ISBN: 978-0-544-07368-5

8 9 10 0908 21 20 19 18 17

4500670288   A B C D E F G

Contents

Vocabulary

environment   producer

ecosystem   photosynthesis

habitat   consumer

Stretch Vocabulary

wetland

mangrove

estuary

Introduction

My name is Dr. Mike Heithaus. I'm a biologist and an ecologist. Ecologists study interactions among organisms and interactions between organisms and their environment. My favorite animals to study are big predators, or animals that hunt prey for food. I'm especially interested in predators that live in the water, such as sharks, dolphins, and alligators.

Some questions I am trying to answer are: How does the environment affect these predators? How do predators find enough to eat? How do predators affect ecosystems they live in? It's important to investigate these questions in order to protect predators and their ecosystems.

To learn about predators, I also have to study the species they interact with and the environment around them. Since 2006, I have been working with teams of scientists to learn about the predators in the coastal Everglades of South Florida.

The Everglades in South Florida includes freshwater marshes (left) and mangrove estuaries (right).

The Everglades

The Everglades is a huge ecosystem that covers southern parts of Florida. It is a wetland ecosystem. Wetlands are places that are covered in water for at least part of the year. Wetlands are very important habitats for many species of plants and animals. They are also important for humans, because they can help clean water, acting like filters that trap harmful particles such as waste and pesticides. The water for the Everglades comes from rivers north of Lake Okeechobee. The water then flows slowly across the state in many channels and shallow marshes.

Shallow freshwater marshes are home to many animals.

Eventually, the water flows into the ocean. Where the fresh water meets the ocean water, estuaries form. Estuaries are places where salt water and fresh water meet.

There are different types of habitats in the Everglades. Each habitat is defined by the kinds of plants and plantlike organisms, or producers, that grow there. Producers are critical to ecosystems. These organisms use water, carbon dioxide, and energy from the sun to make sugar during photosynthesis. The variety of producers that live in an area depends on how deep the water is, how long water is there during the year, the amount of nutrients in the water, and the salt level of the water.

Consumers can't make their own food. They have to eat producers or other consumers. Herbivores are consumers that eat only producers (plants or plantlike organisms). Carnivores are consumers that eat other consumers (animals). Predators are carnivores. One group of consumers breaks down the bodies of dead organisms. These consumers are called decomposers. Without decomposers, nutrients would be lost from ecosystems, and dead material would pile up!

Slow-moving River

There are really only two seasons in the Everglades. The rainy season lasts from May until November. During other months—the dry season—there is very little rain. Everglades marshes are covered by shallow water in the rainy season. During the dry season, much of the marsh dries out.

Sawgrass grows in the marshes. Periphyton also grows there. Periphyton looks like slimy algae, but to many small consumers it is a tasty food—or a great place to live. A sawgrass marsh is a habitat for small fish, grass shrimp, snails, and the birds that eat them. Mangroves, which grow along the shores of estuaries, are a kind of tree that can live in salt water. Small fish and invertebrates live under the roots of the mangrove trees. The roots help protect them from predators. Crabs, turtles, big fish, alligators, crocodiles, and sharks also make the estuary their home.

The Everglades today is very different from what it was hundreds of years ago. Thousands of miles of canals have been built to drain marshes for use as farmland and to help manage the water. The water is managed to prevent floods and for people to use. Much less water flows into the Everglades than used to. But, people are trying to fix the Everglades. To know how much water to let into the Everglades and when to let it in, scientists need to do lots of studies!

The Predators of Shark River

Since 2006, my students and I have been studying the predators in a remote part of the coastal Everglades called Shark River. We want to know how dolphins, sharks, and alligators respond to their environment. This will help us make suggestions about how to restore the Everglades so that these animals are protected. We also want to know how important these predators are to their ecosystem. Do there need to be lots of sharks, alligators, and dolphins around to make sure the estuaries are healthy?

The team has to travel a long way by car and then by boat to get to Shark River. Studying big predators and their environments may be fun, but it is also hard work—especially during the mosquito season. We have to wear special anti-mosquito jackets!

To get to work on Shark River, we have to drive a long way by boat. Sometimes we stay on a houseboat so that we can work day and night!

Why Are Big Predators Rare?

Most people don't know it, but in a lot of places—on land, in the oceans, and in rivers—predators are in trouble. Predators come in all shapes and sizes. Big predators, such as bears and killer whales, are at the top of the food chain. Most big predators eat a variety of different prey animals. Their prey eat many different kinds of foods, too. So, in the real world, there aren't really food chains. There are food webs.

Though they are at the top of food webs, big predators can be hard to find. For example, there are many more deer than there are wolves that prey on them. Why? Animals use up a lot of energy. Most of the energy they take in is used simply to keep their body running. In total, about 90% of the energy consumers take in is lost at every step in the food chain. For every 100 kilograms (kg) of plants, there are only 10 kg of deer produced. For every 10 kg of deer, only 1 kg of wolves is produced! So, it takes many producers to support relatively few consumers. Predators at the top of the energy pyramid have the least amount of energy available to them. That's why the wolf population is much smaller than that of the deer.

Alligators in the Estuary

Most alligators live in freshwater lakes, ponds, canals, and swamps. They can't live in salt water for long because they don't have the special glands needed to pump salt out of their body. But we find alligators living in estuaries, where salt levels can get very high. How they survive in high salt levels is one of the questions we investigate.

The first step in our investigation is to catch alligators. As trained scientists, we have the skills needed to catch alligators while keeping them (and us) safe. To do this, we go out at night and drive up and down the estuary, shining bright spotlights. The light reflects off alligators' eyes, so we can spot an alligator from very far away. When we do find one, we slowly drive up to the alligator and carefully slip a snare over its head. Often, the alligator swims away before we can sneak up on it. But we have a great team and a lot of patience, so eventually we can catch one! Once we've caught an alligator, we tape its mouth shut. Although alligators have strong muscles to close their mouth, they don't have a lot of power to open it, so tape is all we need!

Alligators don't have functional salt glands. How do these animals survive in the salty waters of the mangrove estuary?

Omnivorous Alligators?

We want to find out what the alligators are eating and where they are getting their food. We do this by using water to flush their latest meal out of their stomach and into a sorting tray. It smells terrible!

a typical alligator meal

We have learned some surprising things. First, many of the alligators eat a fruit called pond apples. That means that some alligators are omnivores—they eat both plants and animals. We were also surprised to find that most of the alligators eat small prey, like crabs. If they can, Shark River alligators will also eat birds, turtles, and even smaller alligators. By collecting blood samples and measuring the chemicals in the blood, we found out that some alligators probably grab some of their meals near the ocean. That was a big surprise!

Adam Rosenblatt is the biologist leading the alligator team. Once you catch them, the alligators are usually very calm.

Couch Potatoes and Gators in Motion

How do alligators move through the estuary? How do they respond to changes in the amount of fresh water flowing through the Everglades? To answer these questions, we put special tracking devices on the alligators. The devices allow us to follow their movements. We've tracked one alligator for almost four straight years!

an alligator wearing a tracking device

Not all alligators move and act in the same way. Some alligators stay in the same spot. Others move up and down the estuary. We tagged two alligators close to each other. One seldom left its favorite spot. It must have found enough food right next to the bank it slept on. The other alligator swam hundreds of kilometers to the ocean and back! Wide-ranging alligators like this one probably grab a meal near the ocean. But they can't stay too long because the water is too salty. They swim back upstream to fresher water after they get their food.

The rains affect all the alligators. During the dry season, salt levels increase in the estuary. At this time, even wide-ranging alligators stay upstream because the water near the ocean is too salty.

Freshwater Sharks!

When people think of freshwater predators, they don't often think of sharks. Actually, several shark species can live in rivers. Usually, though, it is young sharks that live in these waters. In Florida, bull sharks can be found in coastal river water that is totally fresh. Shark River is a bull shark nursery. Where do these bull sharks feed? How do they respond to changes in their environment? These are questions we are trying to answer.

We use long ropes to catch bull sharks. We leave these long lines in the water for an hour to see if we have caught a shark. When we catch a shark, we put it in a cooler with water. We measure its length, take a small sample from its fin, and attach a tracking device. We can use the samples to learn about shark diets and to see if sharks get their food from the estuary or from the ocean.

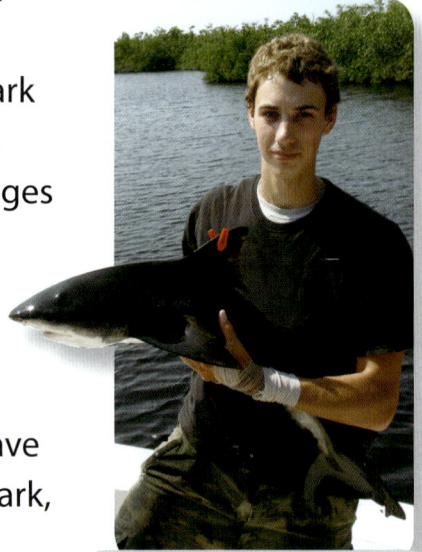

Bull shark team leader Phil Matich holds a young bull shark that is about to be released.

Taking Risks or Playing It Safe

We have discovered that the young bull sharks like to stay far away from the ocean because they are safer there. Where the river empties into the ocean, there are bigger sharks that would eat young bull sharks. But there is also more food for the young bull sharks in the dangerous areas downstream. Some bull sharks play it safe. They stay upstream, where it is harder to get a meal but where they can stay safe. Other bull sharks dare to swim downstream for short periods. They probably take the risk in order to get a good meal. Then they swim back up to where they are safer.

Physical factors of the environment also affect bull sharks. The sharks move around the estuary, trying to find places where there is plenty of oxygen. If the water gets too cold, they have to leave or they could die. Bull sharks will spend their first three to five years in the estuary, and they can handle just about anything from fresh water to full salt water!

Dolphins of the River

Alligators and bull sharks are not the only predators we're studying in Shark River. Team member Robin Sarabia is studying dolphins. Most of the dolphins like to stay near the ocean. That's where there is a lot of food. The dolphins have interesting methods for getting their meals. Sometimes they chase fish onto mud banks. The dolphins slide out of the water, pick the fish off the mud, and wiggle back into the water! Out in the ocean, the dolphins work together to catch fish. During the dry season, when the water gets saltier, some dolphins swim pretty far up the rivers. They swim along the roots of the mangrove trees, looking for fish such as mullet.

We are still trying to find out why some predators travel, while others stay at home. We want to know if the animals that travel for their food are important for bringing nutrients from the ocean up to the producers of the estuary. We will keep studying the large predators of Shark River, so we can better understand and protect the Everglades.

Research a Predator

Choose an ecosystem other than the Everglades to research. Choose a predator that lives there. Research the predator's habitat, diet, and other details about it, such as its traveling range. Create a diagram that illustrates the various aspects of the predator's relationship to its ecosystem. Present your diagram to the class, and explain the various predator/prey relationships you discovered within the ecosystem.

Write a Research Plan

Brainstorm a list of things you would like to know about a particular predator or prey animal. Select one or two questions from your list. Imagine you are a scientist, and create a research plan, using the information in this book as a guide. Explain how you will go about studying the animal in order to answer your questions. Explain what tools you may need, what transportation is necessary, how long your research will take, how many people you need for your plan, and so on. Present your plan to the class.

Glossary

consumer [kuhn·SOOM·er] A living thing that cannot make its own food and must eat other living things.

ecosystem [EE·koh·sis·tuhm] A community of organisms and the environment in which they live.

environment [en·VY·ruhn·muhnt] All the living and nonliving things that surround and affect an organism.

estuary [ES·too·air·ee] The part of the wide lower course of a river where its current is met by salt water.

habitat [HAB·i·tat] The place where an organism lives and can find everything it needs to survive.

mangrove [MAN·grohv] Evergreen salt-tolerant trees or shrubs forming dense thickets along tidal shores.

photosynthesis [foh·toh·SIN·thuh·sis] The process that plants use to make their own food.

producer [pruh·DOOS·er] A living thing, such as a plant, that can make its own food.

wetland [WET·land] A lowland area, such as a marsh or swamp, that is saturated with moisture.